Mr. Sunny Sunshine™

Count, Smile, and Learn.

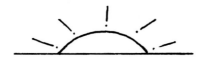

A special dedication of thanks.
To my family and friends who always believed and motivated me from within.
Thanks for your love, smiles, and support.
Here's to you with plenty of smiles.

Yours truly, Dwayne S. Henson...Prince of happiness, King of smiles.

To order additional copies of this book, contact:
Xlibris
1-888-795-4274
www.Xlibris.com
Orders@Xlibris.com

Discover the inspirational magic created from smiles through the guidance of Mr. Sunny Sunshine.

Count, Smile, and Learn.
Written and Illustrated
by
Dwayne S. Henson

Are you ready to smile along with me and count all of the numbers and smiles that you see? The word smile could be hidden anywhere, so we have to look and check everywhere.

Now, let's start our counting with the number one. Do you see the number one and the word smile anywhere? They have to be around here somewhere.

This is the number two. Do you see the word smile anywhere? If you do, can you count how many without me giving you a clue?

3

Three

Smile

Smile

Smile

This is the number three. Hop! Hop! Hop! I have hopped over three smiles exactly. Don't forget to count as you follow me.

4

This is the number four. I am pulling four smiles happily in a wooden wagon. Can you count them all with me? One, two, three, four, smiles.

This is the number five. I am pouring down
five smiles from off a cloud high in the sky.
Can you count them all before they float by?

6

Six

Smile
Smile
Smile
Smile
Smile
Smile

This is the number six. I am leaping over six smiles piled up high and neat. Can you count them all before I land on my feet?

This is the number seven. There are seven smiles somewhere around here. Can you help me find them? We both have to look around and check everywhere.

This is the number eight. Can you count all eight of these smiles before I fly soaring by?

This is the number nine. I now have nine smiles scattered everywhere. We have to count them to make sure that they're all here.

10

Ten

Smile Smile
Smile Smile
Smile Smile
Smile Smile
Smile Smile

This is the number ten. With a wave of this magic wand, I now have ten smiles stacked in two piles nice and neat.

1=One
2=Two
3=Three
4=Four
5=Five
6=Six
7=Seven
8=Eight
9=Nine
10=Ten

Before I go, I would like for you to join me as I count to ten. One, two, three, four, five, six, seven, eight, nine, ten! It was certainly lots of fun counting with you. I hope to count with you soon again.

Coming up next: Tossed and Blown Alphabet...

More smiles coming up...

Tossed
and Blown Alphabet.

Tossed and Blown Alphabet.
Written and Illustrated
by
Dwayne S. Henson

Hello! Hello! I am Mr. Sunny Sunshine, and I'm on another adventure, to where? I don't know. You see I've been tossed and blown far away along with all of the letters in the alphabet from a very bad storm.

Now that I'm back on my feet once again, here's what I aim to do. I'll try to find all of the tossed and blown letters just for you. How about if you come along and help me on this journey too, by pointing out all of the tossed and blown letters that you see.

How about if we start our search for tossed and blown letters over this way? Oh look! Do you see what I see? We found the letters A, B, C, . they were tossed and blown high up into a tree.

Do you see the letters D, E, F, anywhere?
Let's take a look over here. Hey look! Straight
down there, we found the letters D, E, F; they
were tossed and blown right into a very bad
muddy mess.

Look what just went soaring by, it's the letters G, H, and I. The storm tossed and blew them straight up into the sky.

We found the letters J, K, L, down in here!
They were tossed and blown straight into this
wishing well.

Here are the letters M, N, O, P, they were
tossed and blown right into the sea.

We had to look under the sea to find the letters Q, R, S; they were tossed and blown right into a very large treasure chest.

The letters T, U, V, which I almost didn't see, they were tossed and blown on top of a tall hill right behind me.

Hooray! Hooray! Do you see what I see?
It's the last four letters of the alphabet, which
are W, X, Y, and Z. They were strangely
tossed and blown, one on top of each other,
right in front of me.

Now, let's check and make sure we found all of the letters that were tossed and blown away!

- Let's see, we found the letters A, B, C, they were tossed and blown high up into a tree.
- We found the letters D, E, F, they were tossed and blown into a very bad muddy mess.
- We found the letters G, H, and I, they were tossed and blown straight up into the sky.
- We found the letters J, K, L, they were tossed and blown into a wishing well.

- We found the letters M, N, O, P; they were tossed and blown right into the sea.
- We found the letters Q, R, S; they were tossed and blown right into a very large treasure chest.
- We found the letters T, U, V, which I almost didn't see; they were tossed and blown on top of a tall hill right behind me.
- We found the last four letters of the alphabet, which are W, X, Y, and Z. They were tossed and blown strangely one on top of each other right in front of me.

A B C D E F G H I J K L M N O P Q R S T U V W X Y and Z.

Now that we found all of the tossed and blown letters, it's time for me to be on my way. I think there's another storm is headed this way. I hope that you could join up with me soon again on another adventure.

So long for now and have a nice day!

More Mr. Sunny Sunshine books are on the way...

For ordering information Contact
Xlibris at: 1-888-795-4274

Dwayne S. Henson
Creator of Mr. Sunny Sunshine™

My gift that I would like to share with others is to inspire those who are in need of a smile and to educate others of the positive inspirational value that smiles provide in our society.

With Mr. Sunny Sunshine™ as my tool in this never ending educational smile-based journey, I aim to demonstrate how smiles can be utilized in so many positive encouraging ways such as to inspire, motivate, educate as well as to entertain. How Mr. Sunny Sunshine™ creates smiles and shares them with others, I truly believe, are some of the fascinating trademark dynamics of this inspiring smile making concept.

As you may come to discover there's more inspirational magic behind a smile than what we generally see.

From this unique unit of books you'll learn how and why Mr. Sunny Sunshine™ took it upon himself to create more smiles and inspiration all over the world. Along with this you'll also be provided with a one-of-a-kind, entertaining, smile-based education and much, much, more.

There's a lot to uncover and learn about a smile. I invite you to journey along to see how truly motivating a smile can be.

I certainly hope you enjoy my Mr. Sunny Sunshine™ books as much as I did creating them for others to share. I look forward to creating lots more smiles for many of years to come.

Sincerely, Dwayne S. Henson... Prince of happiness, King of smiles.

Printed in the United States
By Bookmasters